For Mum, who loved dogs - P.B.

First published 2021 by Macmillan Children's Books
an imprint of Pan Macmillan
The Smithson, 6 Briset Street, London, EC1M 5NR
EU representative: Macmillan Publishers Ireland Limited,
Mallard Lodge, Lansdowne Village, Dublin 4

Associated companies throughout the world
www.panmacmillan.com

ISBN 978-1-5290-1276-7

Text copyright © Peter Bently 2021
Illustrations copyright © Chris Chatterton 2021

Peter Bently and Chris Chatterton have asserted their rights to be identified as the author
and illustrator of this work in accordance with the Copyright, Designs and Patents Act 1988.

1 3 5 7 9 8 6 4 2

A CIP catalogue record for this book is available
from the British Library.
Printed in China

MIX
Paper from
responsible sources
FSC® C116313
FSC
www.fsc.org

I am Dog!

Peter Bently

Chris Chatterton

Macmillan Children's Books

I am Dog.
Dog is me.

I like walkies.

I see ducks. Ducks on log.

Chasey-chasey!
I am Dog!

Splashy-splashy. Ducks all fly.

Shaky-shaky-shaky dry.

I am Dog. I like race.

I like feeling wind in face.

I like rolls in foxy pong.

Foxy pong is nice and strong.

I like digging.
Scrat-scrat-scrat.

I do NOT like
next-door cat.

I am Dog.
I like cuddles.

I like
lap-lap-lappy
puddles.

I like
scratchy-scratchy
tum.

I like
sniffy-sniffy
bum.

I smell something good to eat.
Tasty-tasty doggy treat.

Sniff-sniff.
Sniff-sniff.

Sniff-sniff.
Where?

Sniff-sniff.
Sniff-sniff.

Sniff-sniff.
There!

Jog-jog. Jog-jog. Jog-jog-jog.
Jump. Hup. Easy!
I AM DOG!

Uh-oh! Can't stop.
Paws won't grip!
Slippy-slidey. Slidey-slip!

Woof!
Yelp!
Crash!

Tumble-tumble!

Oh well. Still here.
Mustn't grumble.

Chomp slurp.
Chomp slurp.
Chomp-chomp slurp.

Lick-lick.
Lick-lick.
Lick-lick —

BURP

I am Dog. Dog is me.
Round and round.
One. Two. Three.

Full tum.
Warm fire.
Sleep like log.

It's a dog's life.
I am Dog.